W9-CSK-811

Attic of the Wind

Attic of the Wind

by Doris Herold Lund

illustrated by Ati Forberg

146515

RETURN TO
CAMPBELL UNION SCHOOL
DISTRICT LIBRARY

Parents' Magazine Press
New York

© Copyright 1966 by Doris Herold Lund
All rights reserved
Printed in the United States of America. Library of Congress Catalog Card Number 65-18657.

146515

What happens to things that blow away,
Like the bubbles you blew one sunny day?
Where did they all go anyway?
To the Attic of the Wind!

It's not an Attic you reach by stair—
It's past the clouds and the stars somewhere!
And what will we find if we play up there
In the Attic of the Wind?

There are autumn leaves that the wind has swirled
From the far-off corners of all the world
And piled up high in a red-gold heap
So hundreds of children can play and leap!

There are all of the snowflakes that didn't light
But whirled past your door on a snowy night.
They didn't melt and they didn't stay—
They're here in the Attic for you today!

There are petals, too, that a daisy sheds,
The fallen blossoms from flower beds,
And the dandelions' soft gray heads—
In the Attic of the Wind!

There are butterflies that flew too high
And lost themselves in the summer sky.

And even one tiny baby wren
Who bravely jumped from his nest and then—
When he tried flying back to his treetop bed
Rode here on a gentle wind instead.

Feathers are here in the Attic, too—
The robin's red and the blue jay's blue,
The peacock's plume and the duckling's down,
And the pheasant's feather of speckled brown.
Feather of gull or of mother quail,
And a green-gold beauty from a rooster's tail!

Balloons in the Attic? Of course there are!
Lost at the Fair or the Church Bazaar.
Balloons from the birthdays of all the years
That you watched float away with a smile...or tears.

And here are the kites that snapped their strings,
Then sailed to the Attic on paper wings!
Red kites from Kansas.
Blue kites from Maine.
Bright yellow kites blown from faraway Spain.
Fish kites from China.
Box kites from France.
Kites from Japan made like dragons that dance!

There are hats blown off of aunts and mothers,
Sailors, policemen, and baby brothers.
Hats for beaching, hats for riding,
Hats for thinking and deciding.
Party hats and paper crowns,
And hats belonging to circus clowns!

RETURN TO
CAMPBELL UNION SCHOOL
DISTRICT LIBRARY

And here in the Attic of the Wind
Is all of the laundry that comes unpinned...
The socks and pajamas that ran away
When a clothesline broke on a gusty day!
The petticoat that whirled off to dance
With a patched-up pair of somebody's pants!

Look here! All the streamers that travelers throw
When a great ship sails and the deep horns blow.
Pink streamers and rice from a wedding day
When the groom takes the beautiful bride away.
Streamers like colored rain coming down
When a hero's parade marches through the town.

And what of umbrellas that disappear
On a stormy day? Why, they're all up here!

Here, too, is that Valentine of lace...
The postcard you got from a far-off place...

...And the golden sparks from a summer fire
That you watched fly high, and then still higher!

Yes, the Attic of the Wind can store
All the world's lost treasure, and even more...
The handkerchief you forgot to hold,
The spelling paper with the star of gold,
The picture you drew for Mother's Day,
All the things you somehow let drift away
Aren't exactly lost. So before you cry—
Why not look in the Attic in the sky?